For Jack, Megan and Ella.

A TEMPLAR BOOK

First published in the UK in 2016 by Templar Publishing,
an imprint of the Bonnier Publishing Group,
The Plaza, 535 King's Road London SW10 0SZ

Copyright © 2016 by Clive McFarland
1 3 5 7 9 10 8 6 4 2

ISBN 978-1-78370-386-9 (Hardback)
ISBN 978-1-78370-387-6 (Paperback)

This title was set in Highlander EF Book, Slappy Inline and Goudy Old Style.
The illustrations were created using crayon, acrylic, watercolour and digital.

Designed by Verity Clark
Edited by Katie Haworth

Printed in China

The Fox and the Wild

Clive McFarland

The Fox and the Wild

Clive McFarland

templar publishing

This is Fred.

He was born in the
middle of a **big** city.

Fred finds life in the city hard. It's smoky.

It's noisy,

and it's very, very fast.

Fred's cousins **love** living in the city.

With Fred, they roam at night when the streets are quiet.

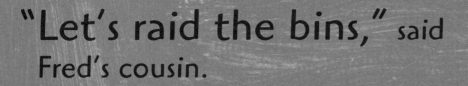

"Let's raid the bins," said Fred's cousin.

"That can be **dangerous**," said Fred.

"It can be **exciting!**" said his other cousin.

But tonight's raid
didn't go as planned . . .

CRASH!
BANG!

yelled an
angry voice.

The foxes fled. Fred's cousins
went one way . . .

. . . and Fred another.

Fred climbed onto a
rooftop to hide.

He was on his own.

Above him, he saw a flock of
birds flying over the city.

"Where do you go?"
Fred called.

But his voice

was carried off

by the wind.

Fred decided to
follow them.

"Where do the birds go?" he asked a tired dog.
"I've never really thought about it," said the dog.

"Have you ever followed the birds?" he asked a skinny cat.
"They get away," said the cat.

"Do they fly beyond the city," he asked a watchful rat.
"There's no such place," said the rat.

Fred wasn't convinced. The city couldn't go on forever.

Suddenly something came tumbling out of the sky.

"honk!"

It was one of the birds.

Fred POUNCED!

"Please, **honk!**" cried the bird, "don't eat me."

"I don't want to," said Fred.

"Have you been where the other birds go?"

"Yes, **honk**. I'm from the wild," said the bird. "Where the trees spread their branches and the wind blows over the hills. You'll never reach it without flying."

"I don't need to fly," said Fred, "I'll hunt!"

And so Fred started to hunt.
"The bird said there are trees in the wild.
I know where to look!"

But this place didn't seem like the wild.

"The wild wouldn't be so bare," said Fred.
"The bird said the wind blows in the wild.
I know where to look!"

But this place didn't seem like the wild.
"The air is too dirty here," Fred choked.

"The bird said there were hills in the wild...
I know where to look!"

But this place didn't seem like the wild.
"The ground is too hard here," said Fred.

He didn't know where to hunt next.

Just then . . .

SCREECH!

CRUNCH!

It was a **metal monster!**
Fred ran for cover.

Inside the
tunnel, it was
too dark
to see.

Fred tried not
to be scared.

Finally he tumbled out
the end and into . . .

. . . trees.

Real **wild** trees. They were greener
than anything he'd ever seen.

Fred trod on wild leaves
and plants.

The ground was softer
than anything he'd
ever walked on.

A wild breeze

swept around Fred.

He'd never smelled anything so wonderful.

Fred heard animals scurrying in the undergrowth.
They sounded better than anything he'd ever heard.

Fred took a breath
of **clean,**
wild air

and **ran** over the **hills.**

He had found it.

"I'm in the WILD!"
he barked.

"Hello," said a voice.

"Do you know where the birds go?"

More picture books from Templar:

ISBN: 978-1-78370-327-2 (hardback)
978-1-78370-328-9 (paperback)

ISBN: 978-1-78370-383-8 (hardback)
978-1-78370-490-3 (paperback)

ISBN: 978-1-78370-238-1 (hardback)
978-1-78370-239-8 (paperback)

ISBN: 978-1-78370-258-9 (hardback)
978-1-78370-259-6 (paperback)